| DATE DUE | | | |
|---|---|---|---|
| | | | |
| | | | |
| | | | |
| | | | |
| | | | |
| | | | |
| | | | |
| | | | |
| | | | |
| | | | |
| | | | |
| | | | |
| | | | |
| | | | |
| | | | |

**31170300100421**
**Zolotow, Charlotte.**

E
ZOL

**Do you know what
I'll do?**

04-117

**DORN SCHOOL MEDIA CENTER**

# Do You Know What I'll Do?

# Do You Know What I'll Do?

## By Charlotte Zolotow

## Pictures by Javaka Steptoe

Revised and Newly Illustrated Edition

HarperCollins*Publishers*

**One day a little girl said to her little brother . . .**

Do you know what I'll do
when the flowers grow again?

I'll pick you a bunch
and you'll be happy.

**Do you know what I'll do
when it snows?**

I'll make you
a snowman.

Do you know what I'll do
when it rains?

I'll catch the rain in a pail
for your plants.

Do you know what I'll do
when the wind blows?

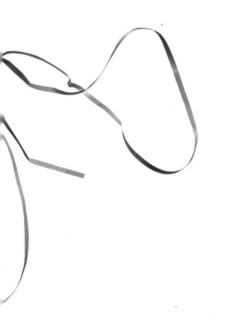

I'll put it in a bottle and let it loose
when the house is hot.

Do you know what I'll do at the seashore?

I'll bring you a shell
to hold the sound of the sea.

**Do you know what I'll do in the city?**

**I'll buy you a surprise.**

Do you know what I'll do at the movies?

I'll remember the song
and sing it to you.

Do you know what I'll do in the night?

If you have a nightmare,
I'll come and blow on it.

Do you know what I'll do at the party?

I'll bring you a piece of cake
with the candle still in it.

**Do you know what I'll do on my walk?**

**I'll look at the clouds and
tell you the shapes when I get home.**

Do you know what I'll do
when I wake up?

I'll remember my dreams and
tell them to you.

Do you know what I'll do
when I grow up and have a baby?

I'll bring you my baby to hug. . . .

Like this!

**To my sister,**
**Dorothy Arnof**
**—C.Z.**

**Dedicated to the millions of children—but especially in Africa—**
**who are being ravaged by a disease called AIDS.**
**What will we do for them?**
**—J.S.**

Do You Know What I'll Do?  Text copyright © 2000 by Charlotte Zolotow  Illustrations copyright © 2000 by Javaka Steptoe
Printed in the U.S.A. All rights reserved.  http://www.harperchildrens.com
Library of Congress Cataloging-in-Publication Data
Zolotow, Charlotte, 1915—
   Do you know what I'll do? / by Charlotte Zolotow ; pictures by Javaka Steptoe. — Rev. and newly ill. ed.
     p.    cm.
   Summary: A little girl delights her brother with a series of promises about all the wonderful things she'll do to make him
happy as they both grow up.
   ISBN 0-06-027879-X. — ISBN 0-06-027880-3 (lib. bdg.)
   [1. Brothers and sisters—Fiction.  2. Growth—Fiction.]  I. Steptoe, Javaka, 1971—  ill.  II. Title
PZ7.Z77Do  2000                                    99-26424
[E]—dc21                                               CIP
                                                          AC

Typography by Al Cetta    1  2  3  4  5  6  7  8  9  10   ❖   Revised and newly illustrated edition

North Palos Dist. 117
Dorn Primary Center
7840 W. 92nd Street
Hickory Hills, IL  60457